CW00406365

The Doctor's Daughter

For Barbara

The Doctor's Daughter

Norma Clarke

Illustrated by Michael Charlton

A & C Black · London

FLASHBACKS

Published 1996 by A & C Black (Publishers) Ltd
35 Bedford Row, London WC1R 4JH

Text copyright © 1996 Norma Clarke
Illustrations copyright © 1996 Michael Charlton

ISBN 0-7136-4394-3

A CIP catalogue record for this book
is available from the British Library.

With special thanks to Noreen Marshall,
Curator of the Dress and Nursery Collections,
at the Bethnal Green Museum of Childhood.

Photoset in Linotron Palatino by
Rowland Phototypesetting Ltd,
Bury St Edmunds, Suffolk

Printed in Great Britain by
St Edmundsbury Press Ltd,
Bury St Edmunds, Suffolk

Contents

· 1 ·

Matty and Eliza

Matty found it easy to jump the broken stile into Back Lane. But before Lane End, where the Porter children lived, there was a muddy ditch, a three-barred gate and a dense patch of nettles to cross. Still, Matty liked to run across the fields. For one thing, nobody would see her and ask why she wasn't wearing her hat or tell her not to run so fast. And for another, she loved the feeling of the wind on her face, especially as she came to the top of the slope before turning down towards the copse of elm and ash that bordered Back Lane.

The Porter family had a new baby and Matty was impatient to see it again.

It was a sunny afternoon in late spring. Matty had been inside all morning, helping Mother sort out clothes for the church bazaar. After lunch she was on her honour to spend half an hour practising the piano, so she duly thumped and banged away in the chilly drawing room. The sun never warmed this room which faced the wrong way, overlooking the road into town. It was rarely used. Father, a doctor, was too busy with his work and experiments and Mother was too busy with her charities for either of them to sit there. Only Matty had to endure it, playing the piano which she hated.

The moment her half-hour was up she slipped from her stool, ran down to the kitchen where Nellie, the housekeeper, was rolling out pastry, and flew out of the back door. Nellie called her back.

'What about your cape?'

Matty quickly unhooked it from its peg.

'And I've a package for you to take to my sister, as well,' Nellie said grumpily. She wiped her hands on her apron and took a package down from the shelf. 'Give this to Eliza's mother.' She looked hard at Matty. 'You look pale. Are you sure you should go out?'

'Quite sure,' Matty said quickly.

A gate at the bottom of the garden gave onto the fields. Once Matty was through this gate, she breathed more easily. Nobody had stopped her. There was always a danger that she would be banned from running over to the Porter children.

There were five Porter children besides the new baby. Arthur, the eldest at thirteen, was now a clerk in the railway office at Norwich so Matty didn't expect to see him. Eliza was Matty's special friend, but Matty liked being with all of them, even Robert who was bad-tempered and sometimes pinched her, and Anna who cried when she didn't get her own way, and Sarah, who used to be the baby. The way they quarrelled and made up enchanted her. It was so different from her own rather polite and quiet home.

Matty scrambled through the nettle patch. She ran across the green and round to the back of the tumbledown cottage. She peered eagerly through the window.

She saw Mrs Porter sitting sewing by the hearth. A small fire was lit. The baby, wrapped in a coarse woollen shawl, lay in a crib nearby.

Matty knocked and went quietly in. Mrs Porter looked up from her sewing. She didn't speak. She was a busy woman most of the time, always at work, and to see her sitting quietly sewing was strange. Her big rough hands looked all wrong holding a scrap of calico and a tiny needle.

Matty handed over the package. 'Nellie said to give you this.'

Mrs Porter took it, thanked her, and put it to one side.

Eliza let Matty pick the baby up. She pulled back the shawl. A little round, red, cross face looked at her. 'She's so lovely,' Matty whispered.

'She can't see properly,' Eliza said. 'Not yet.'

They admired the baby together, wondering at her tiny hands and tiny feet, until Mrs Porter interrupted them.

'Another mouth to feed,' Mrs Porter grumbled. 'Another girl, more's the pity.'

Why is it a pity she's a girl? Matty thought, but didn't dare say.

Eliza spoke softly in Matty's ear. 'Mother's not feeling well today. That's why she's got a fire.'

'Put it down now, don't go dandling it and spoiling it the way Eliza does all the time,' Mrs Porter said. Matty put the baby down at once. She was frightened of Mrs Porter. 'And hurry along with the food, Eliza. Your father and Robert will be half starved.'

Eliza took up a basket covered with a clean cloth. 'You hold this,' she said to Matty, handing her a jug with beer in it.

'Come straight back,' Mrs Porter called out as they went through the door and into the sunlight. 'There's the vegetable patch to be weeded.'

'Yes, Mother,' Eliza said.

The two girls hurried along the broad track. The beer slopped about in the jug. Matty had difficulty holding it, but it amused her to try and do the tasks Eliza did so easily, so long as nobody could see her and so long as she didn't spill the tell-tale beer on her good clothes.

Matty had known Eliza as long as she could remember. Mrs Porter and Nellie were sisters. Eliza had run in and out of Matty's house when she was young, bringing messages for Nellie. Matty, learning her lessons with Mother, would catch glimpses of a dark-haired, cheerful-looking girl not much older than herself, wearing plain country clothes. Then Eliza stopped coming, and Nellie explained that she'd gone to work as a scullery maid for a family called Robinson who lived a few miles away. But Nellie found out that the Robinsons were not treating Eliza kindly. So Eliza came home.

Matty and Eliza became friends when Matty discovered Eliza didn't know how to read. Matty begged to be allowed to teach her. Mother agreed, and Father agreed, but Mr and Mrs Porter didn't see the point.

'It's not as if she'll need it, is it?' Mr Porter had said. 'Not like Arthur.'

All the Porter family were proud of Arthur.

But Matty had insisted. She made up a set of alphabet cards, carefully drawing each letter of the alphabet on a separate card. Her mother helped, and Nellie let her use the kitchen table to lay the cards out and teach Eliza how they joined up into hundreds of different words.

Eliza learned quickly. Soon she could read simple poems and passages from the Bible. Now and again, Matty found an excuse to take a book or little pamphlet over to Eliza. Gradually her visits became longer and more frequent.

The two girls crossed the ditch into the top field. They could now see Mr Porter and Robert, working with some other men and women a little way off. 'I've got a letter from Arthur,' Eliza said. 'I'm going to read it to Father.'

The proud way she said it made Matty smile. Even Mr Porter was glad Eliza could read now.

Robert spotted them. He was cross. 'You're late,' was all he said.

Eliza set down the basket and took off the cloth. Two hunks of bread and two hunks of cheese were neatly placed inside. Matty balanced the jug on a flat piece of earth, glad to be rid of it, and sat down to rest. Mr Porter and Robert took turns to drink from the jug as they ate their bread and cheese.

'Are you going to read the letter?' asked Matty.

Eliza frowned. 'I'm waiting till they've finished,' she whispered, but her father had heard.

'What letter?'

'A letter from Arthur, Father.'

Old Alice, bent double weeding, straightened up to listen. Tom Mercer and Charlie Potts, both the same age as Arthur, also paused and waited while Eliza took the letter from her pocket and opened it up to read aloud. It was a special occasion. Matty silently congratulated herself for choosing *this* afternoon to run over and see the Porter baby.

15

'My dear Father and Mother, and my loving brother and sisters . . .' Eliza began, reading Arthur's letter slowly and clearly.

Matty watched a hare scamper across the border of the field. She envied Eliza. It would be wonderful to be Eliza and have a baby to look after and a brother to be proud of. Lucky Eliza. But Matty felt something else too, a new feeling. It was a sort of restlessness. What if she had been born a boy and could be like Arthur, doing exciting new things?

Eliza read on, her finger following the line of writing. 'Mr Simpson, the works manager, says if I study hard I can go on the footplate and even learn to be a driver . . .'

'A driver!' Robert cried, his eyes shining. 'Our Arthur?'

Eliza continued. 'All the lads go to the Mutual Improvement classes in the evenings after work. We're learning mathematics and all the other things we need to know. Mr Simpson says the railroad is the key to the future, and those of us who are part of it are the luckiest fellows alive.'

Eliza paused. Old Alice had tears in her eyes. 'He's a scholar, that boy,' Old Alice said.

'Did the eggs arrive safe?' Mr Porter asked.

Eliza looked down the letter. 'Yes Father. Arthur thanks you and Mother for that, and he thanks me for mending his shirt. He says he is keeping well and hopes this letter finds us as it left him.'

'It does,' Mr Porter said, nodding gravely. He got up and began working again. 'We've a lot to do before dark,' he said to Robert.

Matty and Eliza didn't talk much as they walked back. Eliza was thinking about her brother. She knew it was wrong to wish him home because he was so happy in Norwich where he had a future and was earning money which the family badly needed. But in the six months he'd been away, she'd grown to miss him more and more. She knew her parents missed him too, though they would never say so. Her father had encouraged Arthur to go. 'There's no future for you here on the land, my boy,' he had said.

Matty was thinking about Arthur, too, but her thoughts were more muddled. She kept forgetting Arthur and thinking about herself and this thing everybody talked about: the future. Did she have a future? What might it be? It was all very hard to work out.

· 2 ·

Strange Voices

When Matty got home, she heard voices coming from Father's study so she didn't go in there. Matty's father, Dr Nelson, was almost always in his study if he wasn't out visiting patients who were too sick to come to him. The study had a desk, several deep leather armchairs, bookshelves crammed with books and – Dr Nelson's pride and joy – a marble bust of a pleasant-looking ancient Greek called Hippocrates.

'Hippocrates is the father of modern medicine,' Dr Nelson had told Matty when she was quite young. 'In a sense, we're all his sons if we choose to be doctors.'

From the study a connecting door led into a surgery, where Dr Nelson treated people with injuries and ailments, and next to the surgery was the dispensary where he made up medicines. Matty never went into any of these rooms without permission. Her greatest joy, however, was to be allowed to stay and watch when Father set up his scientific instruments and did experiments. Dr Nelson could make liquids change colour, he could make them hiss and fizz and bubble through glass tubes. Sometimes he produced foul smells which filled the house and brought Mother and Nellie protestingly to his door.

But ever since Fred and Joe arrived, Matty had been turned away when Father was doing experiments.

Fred and Joe were Dr Nelson's apprentices, two red-faced country lads. They shared the attic room at the top of the house. Matty was shy of them. If she passed them on the stairs she hurried by before they could tease her. During the day

Fred and Joe were kept busy. They studied, helped in the dispensary and sometimes went out with Dr Nelson on his rounds. In the evening, they had lessons with him. Matty had noticed that whereas at first Father had despaired of making anything of them, now he seemed quite proud of what they could do.

Probably, Matty thought, Fred and Joe were doing experiments with Father in his study. What would happen if she knocked at the door and asked Father to let her join in?

Matty went into the kitchen. Nellie was there, chopping mushrooms and onions at the wooden table. Matty could tell, by the way Nellie's eyebrows met and her forehead creased, that she was in a bad mood. Perhaps little Sophie, the new maid, had broken another piece of china. But Sophie seemed happy enough.

'The Porter baby is *so* beautiful,' Matty said, hanging up her cape. Nellie liked babies, too.

Nellie opened the pantry and fetched out a huge lump of raw meat on a marble slab. It was fascinating and horrible to watch as she sliced it into cubes, the blood from the meat turning her palms quite red.

'Another mouth to feed,' Nellie muttered.

'That's what Mrs Porter said!'

'How my poor sister's going to manage I don't know.'

'Arthur's got a good job.'

'He's still only a boy.'

'But he's got a future.' Matty turned the word round and round in her head as she spoke. It seemed to cast a glow upon Arthur.

Nellie snorted. 'Trains? The railroad? That's not the future. That's nothing but foolish noise and mess and trouble. I've seen it with my own eyes and I'm telling you what it is. A dangerous and foolish folly. Why, some of them trains go at thirty miles an hour! It's not natural and it's not healthy.'

'But Father says . . .'

'Your father may know about science and medicine. I'm telling you what's natural and healthy.'

Matty didn't protest. Nellie, in this mood, was never one to be argued with. Something had upset her.

Matty sat silently while Nellie piled the meat into a bowl, sprinkled it with flour, added some

currants and ginger, and rolled out a suet topping. When this was done, she wrapped the bowl in a floured cloth, tied a knot in it and lowered it into a pot of water that was already boiling on the hob.

'I gave Mrs Porter the package,' Matty said at last. 'What was in it?'

'Only some old baby clothes. A bit of cheese. A few scraps of bacon. Don't touch those currants.'

'I expect Mother will go round with some more things.'

'No doubt. She's got something else on her mind at the present.'

This was news to Matty. She wondered what Nellie meant, and why Nellie's eyebrows were so sternly knit together. Mother was generally busy, what with one thing and another, but she was always calm and kind. Matty had seen Nellie get angry with the servant girls, never with Mother.

'Them trains,' Nellie suddenly exploded, 'is causing nothing but trouble. Up and down the country peaceful homes are being rent apart!' She leaned forward. 'Just because you *can* take a train from Norwich to London, doesn't mean you *have* to, does it?'

Matty said, 'No,' and looked at Nellie out of wide, wondering eyes. Her heart started to beat loudly. She had a feeling that something very important was about to happen.

'And how am I going to keep an eye on you if you're all the way away in that dreadful place full of smoke and din?'

'Me?' Matty whispered.

'It's a dreadful place. How your mother can even think about it I don't know.'

'Think about what, Nellie?' Matty breathed.

Nellie handed the marble meat slab to Sophie to scrub. 'Well you know what your father's been thinking about. Your poor mother's been trying to make up her mind for months now. She's got to send you somewhere. You can't spend your whole life playing the piano and running about the fields, can you? Bless you child, you'll be ten this summer. You need a proper education. What kind of a wife and mother will you make if all you know is how to run wild with farm children?'

'I don't want to be sent away!' Matty cried.

'Of course you don't,' Nellie agreed. 'Especially not to London. That's what I said.'

Matty leapt down from the stool. As she did so, Fred and Joe came in the back door from the garden. They were carrying fishing gear. Joe said, 'We caught a pike for you, Nellie. It was *this* big!' He spread his arms as wide as they would go. 'But it got away. We brought you these instead.'

Matty ran headlong out of the kitchen and into the hall.

Voices were still coming from behind Father's study door. If it wasn't Fred and Joe, who *was* Father talking to? Was Mother in there too? Matty had to know. It was wrong to listen to other people's conversations, but she crept up close to the door and put her ear to the keyhole.

It was hard to catch the words. All Matty could make out at first was a murmuring sound. Someone coughed. A chair squeaked. She could tell that both Mother and Father were inside, and at least one other person, for there was a woman's voice she didn't recognise at all.

Then Matty's father said in a matter-of-fact way, 'Of course, we could let you take Mathilda with you. Nellie wouldn't need more than a few days to get her things ready, would she?'

Matty's mother agreed she wouldn't, then added something about a stout pair of shoes.

After some discussion, Matty heard the woman say, 'So that's settled. She'll come with me to London at once. That would be most satisfactory.'

There were some murmurs then which Matty didn't catch. Her heart was beating very fast.

Then there were movements inside Father's study, as if all the people were standing up. Matty fled down the passage. She had done wrong. She had wished for things she didn't have, and that was a sin. She had wanted to be like Arthur who had gone away. Now, like a punishment, her wish had come true. She was to be taken away by a stranger. She had been secretly envious of Fred and Joe, and she had been found out. It was the most frightening moment of Matty's life.

If she went through the kitchen to the back door, Nellie would see her. Matty ran down the short flight of steps towards the front door which she hardly ever used, pulled back the stiff catch, and let herself out on to the public highway.

· 3 ·

Telling Lies to Mr Wilson

She had a stitch in her side and her chest hurt.
Matty stopped running. Ahead was the church
steeple and the big village she had known since
childhood. People knew her there. She was Dr
Nelson's daughter. Beyond was a wooded land-
scape, beyond that Norwich, and beyond that . . .
what? London? Matty shivered. Of course she
would have to turn round and go home. But in the
meantime she stumbled painfully on.

The sound of a horse's hooves clattering made
her start. Perhaps it was Father! The horse and
cart drew level, and Matty saw that it was only
Mr Wilson, the draper.

Mr Wilson drew up beside her. 'Miss
Mathilda,' he said in his jovial way. 'Hop up. I'll
take you. Who are you off to call on?'

Matty said the first thing that came into her
head. 'Miss Ferney.'

'Going to talk about books?'

Miss Ferney was the village schoolteacher, and her cottage was full of books. She taught the village children their letters. She sometimes let Matty borrow one of her precious volumes.

'Yes.'

'Hop up then. Don't want to wear yourself out before you get there.'

Matty climbed up onto the cart. Mr Wilson flicked the reins and they trotted along. Matty really believed for a moment that she *was* going to see Miss Ferney. She hoped Mr Wilson wouldn't ask her too many questions. It was a sin to tell lies.

Mr Wilson pointed with his stubby thumb to the bales of cloth loaded on the cart. 'Best Preston cotton,' he said proudly. 'The finest you can buy. Light but strong. The ladies don't believe me till they feel it. Tell your mother.'

'Yes Mr Wilson.'

'Has she thought about her summer dresses yet?'

'No Mr Wilson, not yet.'

'You tell her to pop in and see what patterns I've got in the store.'

'Yes Mr Wilson.'

'And I've a lovely lot of ribbons to liven up the

old if she doesn't want to buy new. But the fashions are changing. You tell her.'

'Yes Mr Wilson,' Matty said, adding, 'Mother isn't very interested in fashion.'

Mr Wilson laughed so hard his shoulders shook. 'Miss Mathilda,' he said, *all* women are interested in fashion.'

Mr Wilson dropped Matty off at Miss Ferney's gate. He waited.

'Goodbye,' Matty said. 'Thank you.'

A doubtful expression passed over Mr Wilson's face. 'You're sure she's expecting you?'

Matty nodded. A nod was less of a lie. She hoped Miss Ferney was at the bottom of her back garden, out of sight and hearing.

As soon as Mr Wilson clip-clopped away, Matty ran round a clump of trees opposite Miss Ferney's front gate and hid herself in a bank of bushes. She sank with a great sigh of relief onto the dry earth. Then she started crying.

She hadn't meant to wish for what she didn't have. She hadn't meant to tell lies. But it was just as Reverend Dobbs said in church: one sin led to another, and you didn't have to say anything or do anything. It was wicked enough just to think it.

It was a comfort to cry and Matty cried for a good while, quietly at first, then more noisily. It tired her out. She started sniffing. Her eyes were sore. She closed them. Her whole body felt heavy. It was the nicest thing to lie down full length on the bed of dry leaves and know that nobody could see her.

Matty slept. When she woke again it was dark, and Matty found herself looking directly into the face of a woman who was staring at her. The woman had the deepest brown eyes Matty had ever seen. She was wearing a purple cloak.

· 4 ·

The Woman in the Purple Cloak

'You'll feel better now you've slept,' the woman said.

Matty sat up. She rubbed her eyes. 'Who are you?'

The woman smiled. She had a kindly face. It was rather long and a little pale and sad, a face that thought sorrowful thoughts. Mother's expression was like that when she visited old Mrs Bevis whose children all died of the fever within a week of each other.

'I have to go home,' Matty said hurriedly.

'Of course you do.'

'I should never have left. It was wrong and wicked and now it's dark.'

Her voice shook. Matty didn't like the dark.

'It's not so dark,' the woman said. 'Look, there's a moon.'

Between the branches of the trees, Matty could just see the moon, not very high in the sky yet, and looking like a battered silver coin, almost full but not quite round.

'I'll walk home with you. Come.' The woman held out her hand and Matty took it. 'I like to walk in moonlight. See how it washes the stone walls and makes them look blue?'

They stepped from the bank onto the road. The hardness of the stones under her feet told Matty she wasn't dreaming.

'It's wonderful to be able to walk like this,' the woman said. She took a deep breath. 'I love to breathe the clean night air.'

Why? It seemed an odd thing to say. Everybody liked to breathe clean air and Father often walked at night. Sometimes he took Matty with him and pointed out the constellations in the sky.

Matty was puzzled. The woman was well dressed, and by her speech Matty could tell she was a lady. But she didn't sound local. If she lived in their little town or any of the surrounding villages, Mother and Father would have known her.

'Do you live near here?' Matty asked after they had walked a little way in silence.

'Not exactly,' the woman said vaguely, which made Matty frown. Matty hated that sort of answer. She liked things to be clear.

'You must know where you live,' she said sternly.

'I live in London.'

Matty gasped. London? Nellie's words came back to her. *A dreadful place full of smoke and din.* And the woman who had spoken from within Father's study had said something about London. What was it she had said? *I'll take her there at once.*

'London must be a horrible place,' Matty said. An owl hooted. Matty trembled. She looked up at the woman and added, 'I'm not sure I would want to go to London.'

They continued walking down the long road that led from the town to Matty's home. As they reached the top of a slight incline, Matty could see her house. The lamps were lit in the upper rooms. More than anything, she wanted to be at home, inside, warm, safe, with Nellie and Mother and Father.

'I can run home from here,' Matty said. She was calmer now, but she still felt oddly light-headed. 'Thank you for keeping me company.'

Matty ran all the way. She didn't look back. She staggered in at the front door and fell straight into Nellie. Her mother came up.

'Wherever have you been, you naughty child?' Nellie cried.

Before Matty could answer, Mother took her from Nellie's arms.

'Mathilda,' Mother said. 'We thought you were at the Porters.'

'I told you she came back from there in good time, ma'am,' Nellie said.

Mother looked sharply at Nellie. Quietly, she said to Matty, 'Why did you go off like that? I wanted to present you to Miss Carter.'

'Miss who?' Matty looked from Nellie to Mother and from Mother back to Nellie again. Everything was confused. Matty didn't know what to say. She rubbed her eyes because the patterns on the wallpaper suddenly seemed to have started moving.

She heard Nellie say, 'She doesn't look right to me. The child's poorly. I'll make her some hot milk. She should be put straight to bed.'

· 5 ·

Mother

When Matty woke up next morning she had no memory of having been undressed and put to bed the night before. But she was in her nightgown. She was lying with her head on the pillows. Everything was as normal. It was a beautiful sunny morning and birds were singing as they flew in and out of the fruit trees in the garden.

Matty lay quietly listening to the birds for a long time. Distantly, she heard the house going about its daily business. Doors opened and closed. Steps creaked. People spoke. There was the usual coming and going. She had heard such sounds all her life.

Had she dreamed what had happened? Were her parents really going to send her away? What would it be like? Was this how Arthur felt when he knew he was going to Norwich? That woman who had appeared out of the darkness. Who was she?

Perhaps she was a ghost. Father didn't believe in ghosts but Nellie did.

The longer Matty lay in bed, the less she wanted to get up. Her head began to feel strange, as if it wasn't properly fixed to her shoulders. She closed her eyes and felt she was floating. She drifted off into sleep.

'She's a little feverish,' she heard. 'Fetch a basin and sponge.'

Matty knew it was her father sitting on the bed because of the smell of pipe tobacco. She lay still while he sponged her forehead with cool water.

'Father,' she said. 'The lady in the purple cloak . . .'

'Sshh,' said Father. 'You can tell us later.'

'I wanted to ask you if she was real.'

'Not now,' her father said.

Later when Matty woke her mother was beside her. Matty sat up. 'I'm hungry,' she announced.

She was thirsty, too. When she'd had a drink of water and some bread and butter she leaned back on her pillows and told her mother all she could remember of what had happened.

'Who was that woman, Mother?' she asked. It had tired her out to remember and tell.

'I suppose it must have been Miss Carter,' Matty's mother said. 'She's staying at the inn for a few days. I must send Nellie with a note to thank her for looking after you.'

'And is Miss Carter a teacher?'

'Yes. Miss Carter runs a little school for girls in London. Father thought perhaps it might be suitable for you.'

Matty nodded and said nothing. There were many confusing thoughts in her head. Was Mother right? Was the lady who had found her the same person who had been in Father's study? Their voices weren't at all the same. Matty felt foolish for running away and being afraid. It was wrong to listen to Nellie. Nellie was only a servant and didn't understand. What could Nellie know about a great capital city like London?

Mother sat very still and straight, with her hands resting on her lap. They were fine, white hands. She wore one amber ring and a silver and pearl bracelet. Matty adored her – everybody did. She was beautiful and kind and took an interest in everybody's concerns. All the poor people in the village knew Dr Nelson's lady would look out for them. When winter came, there would be blankets and soup. Matty had always hoped she would be like her when she grew up.

'Mother,' Matty said anxiously. 'Why does Father want to send me away? Is it because I ask too many questions?'

'Dear child!' Mother exclaimed in surprise.

'Nellie said . . .'

Mother hushed her. She thought for a moment, then she said, 'Father has been anxious about your education for some time.'

'But you teach me,' Matty cried. 'And Father teaches me all sorts of things. At least, he used to, till Fred and Joe came.'

'Father feels that a proper school, run by respectable, well-educated women, will give you the best preparation for life. You need to be with girls of your own class in society.'

Matty knew what Mother meant. She meant there had been too much running around with the Porter children and being friends with Eliza.

'Father heard about Miss Carter's school from Reverend Dobbs,' Mother went on. 'Reverend Dobbs has been corresponding with Miss Carter for years. Sometimes they write in Greek. Miss Carter teaches Greek to her girls.'

'I thought only boys learned Greek,' Matty said, frowning. Fred and Joe had teased her by reciting lists of medical words in Greek.

'And, of course, you will learn more than I could possibly teach you about history, geography, poetry. Your deportment . . .'

'Deportment . . . ?' This was a new word to Matty.

Mother explained how important it was to know how to stand still and straight, how to answer simply and sensibly when people spoke to you.

'Do I have to go away to learn these things? Why can't I have lessons with Miss Ferney?'

Mother smiled. 'Miss Ferney can't prepare you for your station in life. Miss Ferney teaches the village children.'

'Or with Reverend Dobbs?' Reverend Dobbs had three scholars in his house, just as Father had his apprentices.

Mother shook her head. 'If you were a boy,' she said, 'it would be so much easier.'

'Why?'

'Father would take you on as his apprentice, of course. He would teach you everything he knew.'

'Is Father sorry I'm not a boy?'

Mother was unprepared for this question. Matty sensed that it had pained her and wished she could call the words back. Perhaps Mother had wanted to have a son? Matty would certainly have liked to have had a brother. It was dull being an only child.

'Father has Fred and Joe,' Mother said. 'And we have our part to perform as women, which God has put us here to do.'

Mother reached out and took Matty's hand. She spoke very solemnly. 'Remember,' she said, 'we have to be an example to others less fortunate than ourselves. We have our duties.'

How simple and how glorious everything would have been, Matty thought, if only she had been born a boy. She could have studied with Father, learning everything he knew, and when she grew up she could have been a doctor like him.

'I know it's hard to leave home,' Mother said. 'But you are also fortunate. Not every girl is given such an opportunity and you must use it wisely. You must be good and brave as a boy would be.'

A boy wouldn't be frightened about going away to school. He would be excited. There was so much to learn. He would write letters home just like Arthur's. 'Hoping this finds you as well as it leaves me . . .'

'Mother,' Matty said, 'do you ever wish for things you can't have?'

'No darling,' Mother said firmly. 'That would be quite wrong. You must sleep now. You're getting feverish again.'

Next morning, Matty woke feeling stronger. Mother sat with her while she ate her breakfast.

'Will there be many other girls at the school?' Matty asked.

'Quite a few,' Mother said. 'I believe Miss Carter said she had eight or nine girls at the moment. Of course, that could change at any time.'

'How long will I stay?'

'A year? Two? We'll see how you get on. Of course you'll come home for holidays and we'll come and visit you sometimes.'

Matty said thoughtfully, 'I'll be like Arthur.'

'Like Arthur?' Mother didn't look pleased. 'You won't be a bit like Arthur. How could you be? He's a rough country boy learning to be an engine driver. We're sending you to school so that you will become an accomplished lady.'

Mother got up. 'I must write that note for Nellie,' she said in her businesslike way. 'And I'll ask Miss Carter to tea and see if she can stay until you're better and then you can travel down to London with her.'

But before that could be arranged, something happened which interrupted all their plans.

· 6 ·

Stolen!

The following afternoon, Mr Wilson, the draper, pulled up outside the house. Mother was putting her hat on to go out.

Mother said, 'Oh, Mr Wilson, it is kind of you to call, but I'm not quite ready with my order yet.'

'Have you heard the news, ma'am?' Mr Wilson said. 'All the ladies are talking about it. About the Porter baby.'

'What about the Porter baby?' Matty cried.

Matty's fever had gone. She had been allowed to sit with Nellie in the kitchen.

Mother looked anxiously at Matty, then at Mr Wilson.

'What about the Porter baby?' Mother said. 'Is she sick? Shall I tell the doctor?'

'I'll get Father,' Matty said.

'Not sick,' interrupted Mr Wilson. 'Stolen.'

He leaned back, pleased by the effect of his news. 'Stolen by that lady that was wandering about in the fields. Imagine! The wickedness of folk!'

'That's impossible!' Mother said.

'Stolen and gone,' repeated Mr Wilson in a satisfied way. 'And how will they ever find her again now she's taken? Still, it's one less mouth to feed, eh?'

He flicked the reins and clip-clopped away into town. Matty decided she didn't like Mr Wilson at all, even if it was a sin to bear ill-will in her heart.

'That's a wicked thing to say!' Matty cried. 'Mother, I don't understand. Why should anybody steal the Porter baby?'

Mother was as confused and upset as Matty. Nothing of the sort had ever happened before. Nellie came from the kitchen and joined them in the hall. At the sound of so many raised female voices, Father, Joe and Fred also appeared.

Mother tried to speak calmly but her eyes were wet and her cheeks flushed. She explained to Father what Mr Wilson had said. Father at once told Joe to saddle his horse so he could ride to the Porter cottage.

'Let me come with you, Father!' Matty begged.

It was out of the question. Matty had to watch as Father put on his boots and collected his things.

What had Mr Wilson said? Matty remembered waking up near Miss Ferney's cottage. The lady in the purple cloak had been kind to her. Could that lady have stolen the baby? Why was she wandering around alone at night?

And besides, when Matty had asked Mother who the lady was, hadn't Mother said she was Miss Carter?

When Father returned a few hours later, he brought Eliza with him.

Matty had heard Father explain to Mother, 'It wasn't the child's fault. But Mrs Porter can't stop reproaching Eliza. I brought her here on the pretext of giving her a special medicine.'

'She can stay as long as she likes, poor thing,' Mother had replied.

Matty was allowed to take Eliza out into the conservatory. 'It was all my fault,' Eliza said. Her face was blotched from weeping.

'Don't cry,' Matty said, crying.

'It makes me feel better,' Eliza sobbed.

After a bit, they dried their eyes and Matty asked Eliza to tell her what had happened.

They sat side by side on a wicker sofa. All about them were bright spring plants in pots. The sun sparkled on the glass of the conservatory and warmed them through. Even so, Eliza kept shivering.

'I only put the baby outside on the grass. The sun was so warm and it must be good for her.'

Eliza had to stop then and give way to another fit of weeping. 'Oh, I hope she's safe!' she wailed. 'If only she's safe!'

'Did you see anybody?'

'Nobody. Nobody.'

'Mr Wilson said there was a woman wandering about in the fields . . .' Matty said.

'I saw nobody,' Eliza insisted. 'There weren't no strangers on the lane nor in the fields. Only Miss Ferney came up in the morning for some milk.'

'Eliza,' Matty said. 'There's something mysterious about all this. I don't understand it.'

'There's nothing to understand,' cried Eliza. 'The baby is stolen. She's gone and that woman they saw is gone too.'

Matty said nothing. She thought about a conversation she once heard between Father and Nellie. Father had been explaining about science and scientific proof. Nellie, obstinate as always, wouldn't listen. Father never took offence at Nellie, for he'd known her all his life. Nellie clapped her hand to her heart and said, 'You may prove this and you may prove that with your experiments, but I know by *this* – ' and she gave her chest a great thump – 'if a thing is right or wrong.'

Matty didn't know why she should suddenly remember this conversation. But, like Nellie, she had a feeling. She knew deep inside that no matter what people were saying, or how certain everything seemed, something was wrong. Matty had seen and spoken to the lady in the purple cloak. *She* wouldn't have stolen anybody's baby!

'Eliza,' Matty said gently. 'We shouldn't just sit here and cry.'

Tears streamed down Eliza's face. 'What else can we do?'

'We must make ourselves useful,' Matty said. 'We must go and find the baby, and bring her home where she belongs.'

· 7 ·

Meeting Miss Carter

'They sell babies to the rich folk in London,' Nellie was saying. 'In London the food's so bad it poisons the rich folks and they can't have their own babies. So they come up into the country and steal healthy country babies. It's a sin. It's a wicked sin. God will punish them.'

Everybody was blaming the strange lady who had been seen in the village. Matty was worried. The only stranger she had seen was the woman who had worn the purple cloak. Could she have taken the Porter baby? And could she possibly be Miss Carter? There was only one way to find out. Mother had said Miss Carter was staying in the village for a few days. They had to go and find her.

Matty turned to Eliza. 'Come on. We must go into the village quickly.'

'Why?' Eliza, limp and miserable, hung back.

'Come on,' Matty said. 'I'll explain as we go.'

She took Eliza's arm in hers and the two girls

slipped out.

They soon came to the village. They passed Miss Ferney's cottage. All the curtains were closed. They passed Mr Wilson's drapery shop. A knot of women stood on the verge gossiping. When one of the women called out, 'It's Eliza Porter! Hey, Eliza Porter! Stop! Have they found your baby yet?' Eliza bent her head and ran away.

At the inn they asked Mr Browning, the inn-keeper, if they could send a message up to Miss Carter.

'Is it about the baby?' Mr Browning asked.

'Yes,' Matty replied.

'Terrible business,' Mr Browning said. 'Did you ever hear of such a thing?'

'No,' said Matty. Eliza was too miserable to speak.

Miss Carter said she would receive them in her sitting room on the second floor of the inn. Mr Browning led them up. The stairs were of pol-ished wood. As they climbed them, Matty counted each one. It was as if she was counting the steps to her doom. If Miss Carter *was* the woman in the purple cloak . . . What then?

The door opened and the two girls found

themselves facing a pleasant-faced, plump, pink-cheeked, fair-haired and blue-eyed woman wearing a neat grey wool dress, who rose and crossed the room to greet them politely.

Matty cried out with relief, 'So you're not the woman in the purple cloak!'

'Good heavens!' said Miss Carter. 'Purple? I only ever wear grey and black.'

Eliza said tearfully, 'Please, Miss. Have you heard about our baby? If you know anything, I beg you'll tell us. We're worried sick. Mother's worried sick about the baby.'

'What baby?' Miss Carter said.

'Our new baby that's stolen. I only put her out on the grass to enjoy the air and now she's gone and it's all my fault.'

Miss Carter looked from one girl to the other.

Matty said, 'It wasn't Eliza's fault.'

'I'm so sorry,' Miss Carter explained. 'But I haven't the faintest idea what you're talking about. Would you like to sit down and tell me?'

The girls sat side by side on a small sofa. Miss Carter rang for Mr Browning and ordered lemonade to be brought up.

'I've been reading and writing in my room all day,' Miss Carter explained while Mr Browning poured the lemonade from a jug. Eliza's hands shook when she tried to drink.

'Terrible business,' Mr Browning said.

Miss Carter waited for Mr Browning to leave the room. It was clear he wanted to stay and talk, and even clearer that she wasn't going to invite him.

The lemonade was fresh and sweet. Matty drank a whole glass. She put the glass carefully back on the tray. She was aware that Miss Carter was watching her. Matty could tell that Miss Carter was the sort of person who noticed everything.

'Now,' said Miss Carter. 'What is this about a baby and a purple cloak?'

Both girls began speaking at once. Miss Carter raised her hand. 'One at a time please,' she said.

'You tell her.' Eliza shrank back in the seat.

'The baby was stolen from outside Eliza's house,' Matty began. 'But it wasn't Eliza's fault.'

'I only turned my back for a minute,' Eliza interrupted.

'And the only person it could have been was the woman in the purple cloak. She must have been staying in the village!'

'She took our baby,' Eliza cried. 'Everybody says so.'

'Ah.' There was a pause. Miss Carter looked at them kindly. 'Your poor mother,' she said to Eliza. 'I hope someone is caring for her.'

'Father went straight over,' Matty said.

'Father?'

'Dr Nelson,' said Eliza, as if Miss Carter should have known.

Miss Carter again said, 'Ah.' Then she fixed Matty with a thoughtful look. 'So you must be Mathilda. I had been hoping we would meet earlier.'

'Yes,' said Matty. 'I'm sorry.' She blushed. It was all muddled and wrong to be meeting Miss Carter this way, but it simply couldn't be helped.

'Well now, curiously enough,' Miss Carter said, 'there *was* a lady here who answers your description. I did meet her.'

'Who was she?' Matty cried. 'I'm sure she wouldn't do anything bad.'

Eliza leapt to her feet. 'Where is she now?'

'Her name was Miss Towers,' Miss Carter went on. 'But where she is now, I don't know. I had a most interesting conversation with her when I first arrived. After that I didn't see her. I have been busy preparing some lectures for my top girls.'

'What did she tell you?' Matty asked.

'She told me that she was born in this neighbourhood. Unfortunately her parents died and she was sent to live with distant relations in London. She had a sister who was adopted and brought up by a good family here. What she didn't tell me, but what I can tell you, is this: I am sure she did not snatch anybody's baby.'

Miss Carter folded her hands in her lap and sat very still.

'How do you know?' Eliza cried. 'And if she didn't, who did? She must have. Why has she run away?'

Miss Carter looked at Eliza kindly. 'You're upset,' she said. 'It's natural. We must put our heads together and think about this intelligently. What makes you think she's run away?'

'Everybody says so.'

'Ah,' said Miss Carter, and smiled.

Matty sat silently while Eliza sniffed and Miss Carter added, 'I am quite convinced Miss Towers did not take your baby. However, I'm not convinced she cannot tell us something about it.'

Both girls took a moment to understand this.

'Do you think she saw something?' Matty asked.

Miss Carter said, 'Possibly. Or rather, I think she actually came here because she feared something of the sort might happen.'

'But how would she know? How could she?'

Eliza, who had been trying not to sob, now started crying again. 'Do you mean there was a gang all planning to steal our baby?' she wailed. 'That's horrible!'

'No,' Miss Carter said. She got up from her seat and came and sat beside Eliza. She gently stroked her hair as she spoke. 'When I spoke to Miss Towers, she told me a little about why she had come here. She said she was deeply troubled about a close relative of hers. She didn't tell me who it was. She said she had come to be near her and watch over her in case she should be needed.'

'A female relation?' Matty asked.

'Yes.'

'Living here?'

'Apparently.'

'And she was watching over her?'

'So she said.'

Eliza stared at Miss Carter in astonishment.

Matty sprang from her seat.

'*That's* how she came to be there the other night! *That's* how she found me!'

'Explain to us,' Miss Carter said calmly.

'Outside Miss Ferney's cottage!' Matty cried. 'I fell asleep outside Miss Ferney's cottage.'

'You fell asleep?' Miss Carter said. 'Isn't that rather a strange thing to do?'

Matty blushed. She liked Miss Carter. It embarrassed her to remember how she had run away after listening at her father's study door and how she had been so afraid. Now she had met Miss Carter she wasn't afraid any more.

'When I woke up, she was standing over me.'

'Miss Towers?'

'Yes. And she was very kind to me.'

'That was the impression I had formed of her,' Miss Carter said.

Eliza, wretchedly twisting a handkerchief in her lap, cried out, 'But what about our baby? If she didn't take her, who did?'

Miss Carter stood up. 'Shall we go and call on this Miss . . . What did you say her name was, Matty?'

'Miss Ferney,' Matty replied.

'Yes,' Miss Carter said decisively. 'Let us pay a call on Miss Ferney.'

· 8 ·

Solving the Mystery

Holding each girl by the hand, one on each side of her, Miss Carter led the way down the village street. She chatted as they went. She asked Eliza about the other members of her family and listened to all Eliza had to say about her brothers and sisters.

'And what about you, Mathilda?' she said brightly. 'Like me, you are a doctor's daughter.'

'Yes,' Matty answered politely, not sure what to say.

'Don't you think medicine is the most exciting profession imaginable in our times? Does your father talk to you about it?'

Miss Carter waited for an answer. None came. Ever since Fred and Joe arrived and started living in the house as Father's apprentices, medicine, for Matty, had meant the closed door of Father's study. She was a girl.

'If I was younger,' Miss Carter said, 'if I was,

like you, born into this wonderful era of progress and advancement, I think I would devote my life to medical science.'

Matty looked up. Miss Carter's eyes were shining. Her pink cheeks glowed. Matty said, 'Do you mean, if you had been born a boy?'

Miss Carter stopped. She stood stock still in the road. Matty tripped over her own feet and even Eliza, much sturdier than Matty, stumbled.

Miss Carter said, 'No. I do not mean that at all.'

'But girls can't want to be doctors,' Matty said. It made her very bitter to say it. She wished it wasn't true.

'Why not?' said Miss Carter.

'They're not allowed,' Eliza said. 'It's not right.'

'Why not?' Miss Carter said again. 'Is it so unthinkable? This is the nineteenth century, you know. The age of progress.'

They walked on. Eliza said, 'Only men can be doctors, isn't that right?'

Miss Carter said triumphantly, 'Our women are doing wonderful things all over the world. Look at Miss Nightingale! What an example she has been! If women can be nurses now – and such splendid nurses – why shouldn't they be doctors in the future?'

Matty thought these were the most exciting words she had ever heard anyone say.

'And everybody knows about the courage of Grace Darling. Another example! She was merely a girl, but she trusted God and went out in that dreadful storm.'

'She rescued the shipwrecked mariners,' Eliza said. 'We read about it, didn't we Matty?'

At that moment, they arrived at the gate to Miss Ferney's cottage. The front door opened. Nobody came out at first, but a woman could be seen inside. She was wearing a purple cloak.

'That's the woman I spoke to!' Matty cried.

Matty and Eliza both made to run forward but Miss Carter had hold of their hands and she stopped them.

'Don't run,' she said sternly. 'And don't shout.'

The woman wearing the cloak – Miss Towers – came out into the sunlight. Behind her, looking pale and sad, stepped Miss Ferney. Miss Towers was holding something under her cloak. With her free hand, she guided Miss Ferney along the little path. Miss Ferney's eyes were downcast, and Miss Towers was preoccupied. They didn't notice the trio standing at the gate.

A crying sound came from under Miss Towers' cloak.

'The baby!' Matty exclaimed.

'It's our baby!' cried Eliza.

Miss Ferney gasped. She seemed about to fall. She leaned on the gate for support.

To Matty's astonishment, Miss Towers said quickly, 'My sister didn't mean any harm!' while Miss Ferney whispered, 'I'm so sorry . . .'

Miss Towers pulled back her cloak. Lying snugly in the corner of her arm was the baby herself. Eliza reached out for her and pressed the baby close to her. She turned to Miss Ferney and looked at her with real hatred.

'Why did you take our baby?' she cried. 'That was a wicked, wicked thing to do!'

'I didn't mean to,' Miss Ferney said quietly. 'I only borrowed her. I thought, as your mother had so many, she might not mind too much . . .'

Her voice faded away. She clutched at Miss Towers as if she might faint.

Miss Towers said, 'Hush, sister. All will be well.'

'I thought,' Miss Ferney whispered, 'if I took her, I could give her a better start in life. But I didn't mean to steal her. I was going to ask Mrs Porter . . . Only my courage failed. And then I don't remember what happened. I found myself at home in my cottage with the baby in my arms.'

Miss Ferney burst out crying. Eliza frowned. 'It was a wicked thing to make us worry so. Poor Mother has been beside herself. *And* she's been ill, too. I hope God will forgive you for what you've done to her.'

Eliza put the baby comfortably against her shoulder and quickly took a few steps away from all the others as if she feared they might try to snatch the baby from her again.

'We were just on our way to return her,' Miss Towers said.

'I'm taking her straight back to Mother,' Eliza said fiercely.

Without another word, she turned and set off for home. Miss Carter called out to Eliza but she didn't seem to hear.

Miss Carter looked anxiously after her. 'Will the child manage with the baby?'

'Eliza has always looked after the babies,' Matty explained.

'Of course,' said Miss Carter.

Matty hopped from one foot to the other, uncertain what to do. Eliza was stomping towards the stile that led across the fields to Back Lane. Miss Ferney was being led back into her house. Miss Carter insisted she should be put to bed at once. 'Perhaps your father will come and see her later?' she said over her shoulder to Matty. Matty had stayed on the road side of the gate.

'I'll tell him,' Matty called out.

She had decided what to do. She ran off at once towards the stile, going as fast as she could in order to catch up with Eliza.

· 9 ·

Father

The Porter cottage was crowded with people. Dr Nelson was there, and Joe and Fred. Arthur had come from Norwich. Mr Porter and Robert were talking earnestly with Arthur on one side of the hearth and Nellie and Mother comforted Mrs Porter on the other. When Eliza and Matty appeared in the doorway, holding the baby, nobody noticed them at first.

'Mother,' Eliza said.

As soon as Mrs Porter saw what Eliza was carrying, she gave a cry and got up. There was a sudden silence. Everybody turned to look.

Arthur said, 'It's Baby! She's back! Eliza found her! Hooray for Eliza!' and threw his cap in the air. As the cottage was low, the cap hit the ceiling and fell straight down onto Arthur's nose, confusing him for a moment.

Then the hubbub broke out more loudly than before. Questions and exclamations filled the air.

Mother, Mrs Porter and Nellie were all crying with relief. Dr Nelson and Mr Porter had tears in their eyes and Matty noticed Joe quickly ducking his head to mop his face with his sleeve.

'It was all a mistake about the lady in the purple cloak, Father,' Matty explained to Dr Nelson. 'It was Miss Ferney who took the baby, and she isn't at all well. She took the baby but she didn't mean to. She won't be punished, will she, Father? Can you go over and see her? Miss Carter asked if you would.'

'Goodness me,' Dr Nelson said. 'What a lot you've achieved, Matty. Yes, I'll go and see her later.'

The press of bodies in the tiny cottage, the volume of noise from so many voices, all talking at once and all happy at last, gave Matty a headache. She was tired.

'Can we go home now, Father?' she said. 'Can I ride with you?'

Dr Nelson looked at her and said, 'I think we'd better.'

After a quick word with the Porters, Dr Nelson took Matty and hoisted her up onto his horse. He got on behind. They trotted slowly home by the

road and Matty explained to him as clearly as she
could all that had happened.

When they reached home, Dr Nelson said, 'Let's have tea in my study.'

'But Nellie's not here,' Matty said.

'Then we'll have to get it for ourselves.'

Father assembled everything onto a tray. It was strange to see him in the kitchen, filling the kettle and putting it on the hob just like Nellie – but not quite in the way Nellie did it. Matty felt more comfortable once they had gone into his study. She settled herself happily in one of the leather armchairs.

'Father,' Matty said, 'did you ever wish I had been born a boy?'

Dr Nelson was so surprised by the question that he spluttered over his tea. 'Whatever gave you that idea?' he said. 'How could I wish you to be other than you are? I thank God every day for blessing me with such a fine daughter.'

'What I mean is,' Matty went on, blushing and feeling nervous, but she needed to say what was in her mind, even if it was – as usual – a series of questions. 'Don't you wish I had been a boy, so that you could teach me medicine, the way you teach Joe and Fred? Don't you wish I could have been a doctor just like you?'

Dr Nelson looked a little alarmed. 'Goodness me, no. Do *you* wish that?' he said.

'No, Father,' Matty said quickly. It was wrong to wish for what you couldn't have. 'Only . . .'

'Only what?'

'Only, Miss Carter said . . .'

Father smiled. 'Miss Carter is a remarkable woman,' he said. 'She has vision.'

'What's vision?'

'Vision is when you can see the shape of the future. Sometimes, by believing something strongly enough, people with vision help make it happen.'

'Tell me more about Miss Carter, Father,' Matty said. It was wonderful to have all Father's attention to herself at last.

'Miss Carter has advanced ideas,' Dr Nelson said. 'She thinks women will one day do all the things men do. She believes they will be doctors, and lawyers, and members of parliament. Why, I think she even supposes women can be ministers in God's church.' Dr Nelson laughed kindly. 'Who knows what women will do? It is *my* view that it won't happen, and it wouldn't be right, but I like a woman of sense and spirit and I like Miss Carter. She will take good care of you and prepare you for the future.'

Father buttered himself another slice of fruit-bread and munched it contentedly.

'Why wouldn't it be right, Father?' Matty asked.

'Because women have a duty to care for others,' Dr Nelson said. 'We all have our duties.'

Matty thought about that. Of course it was the duty of all women to care for others, as Mother did. But something else struck her.

'Father,' she said. 'You care for others, too. You're a doctor.'

'That's very different,' Father replied. 'Now eat up. You've hardly touched your bread and butter.'

'What is the difference?'

Father frowned. 'It's just different,' he said. 'A doctor is a professional person. A doctor is medically trained. He has scientific knowledge.'

'Couldn't a woman have scientific knowledge and know all about medicine?' Matty asked, thinking about what Miss Carter had said.

'Not in the same way,' said Father.

Matty saw that he was beginning to be an-

noyed. Soon he might say, 'Too many questions!'
She said no more, but quietly ate and drank and
enjoyed being alone with Father in his study.
Father was the kindest father anyone could have.
He knew all sorts of clever things.

But perhaps there were some things Father
didn't know. Perhaps these were things which
other people – like Miss Carter – knew. And one
day Matty might know them as well.

· 10 ·

Moving On

Matty's portmanteau was packed and stood ready in the hall. Miss Carter was having a last word with Dr and Mrs Nelson in the drawing room. It had been arranged that Arthur, who was due back in Norwich that afternoon, would travel with them in the coach.

Nellie had fussed and fretted all the day before. Now she stood with her arms folded, her red-rimmed eyes fixed on Matty. 'You look so grown up in that new coat,' she said. She reached for her handkerchief and blew her nose hard.

'Nellie,' Matty said, 'I'm coming home again in three weeks' time.'

'It won't be the same,' Nellie sniffed. 'It's the end of an era.'

Matty didn't want to think of it like that. For her it was an adventure. She was travelling towards a future. Mother and Father had made sensible plans. They had worked out that she could come home after three weeks for a break, and if she was happy at school she could go back for another six weeks. Then it would be summer and they were making arrangements to go to the continent. Father wanted to visit a German scientist he had been exchanging letters with.

Mother and Father both kissed Matty tenderly as she prepared to climb into the coach. Nellie wept. Joe and Fred grinned and waved.

'Write at once,' Mother called out. Matty noticed with surprise that Mother was dabbing her eyes with a lace handkerchief.

'I will,' Matty said, as Mr Day clicked the reins and the horses moved slowly off. There was a new writing case in her portmanteau purchased specially for that purpose.

Miss Carter settled back in her corner. Matty hung out of the window waving until they went round the bend in the road and the house disappeared.

Suddenly, Matty felt cold.

'Come and sit by me,' said Miss Carter.

'Father is going to see Miss Ferney again later today,' Matty said. It comforted her to know that the usual routines would go on even though she wouldn't be there.

'Poor Miss Ferney,' said Miss Carter. 'But it is a blessing, the way good comes out of evil.'

Matty said, 'I don't think anybody was evil, do you?'

'No,' said Miss Carter. 'But Miss Ferney was very unhappy, and now Miss Towers will take care of her.'

Mr Day pulled up outside the Porter cottage. Arthur was waiting on the grass verge with a parcel of clean linen under his arm. Eliza stood framed in the doorway, holding the baby. Mrs Porter came out and took the baby from Eliza.

Matty suddenly whispered, 'And Mrs Porter was disappointed her baby was a girl. And now she knows how precious she is.'

Miss Carter smiled. Arthur climbed in, taking off his cap as he did so and stuffing it into his jacket pocket.

'Goodbye Eliza,' Matty said. 'I'll come and see you the moment I come home from school in three weeks.'

'Good luck,' Eliza said.

They pulled away, and Arthur said, 'She might not be here, you know. Eliza's going into service.'

'Eliza?' Matty was shocked. She had been feeling so grown up about going away to school, so pleased at herself for not blubbing and hanging onto Nellie's skirts. Arthur's words changed everything.

Arthur nodded. 'It's all fixed up,' he insisted.

Matty wanted everything at home to stay exactly the same. She wanted the Porter children to be in their cottage as they'd always been.

'Eliza can't go into service,' Matty exclaimed, glaring at Arthur. 'Look what happened last time.'

'That was just bad luck. But when Mr Simpson told me they needed a good kitchen maid at the Hall, a strong sensible girl like Eliza, I told Father.

It's only fair. Everybody has to help. If she's careful she'll be able to send a bit of money back, like I do.'

'Where is the Hall?' Matty asked glumly.

'In Norwich. I'll be able to keep an eye on her.'

'How will your mother manage?'

'Anna's big enough to help now,' Arthur replied. 'She won't learn if 'Liza's there to do everything, will she?'

Nellie was right after all. It *was* the end of an era. Matty looked out over the fields and felt, for the first time, a sadness at leaving. But it didn't last long. As they came in sight of Norwich and Arthur chattered about his job on the railway and his hopes for the future, Matty cheered up.

'Is it really dirty and smelly and smoky and noisy in London?' she asked Miss Carter.

'Not where we shall be. Our school is in Tottenham, a pretty village to the north of London.'

'And how do you think I'll get on there?'

'I think you'll get on very well,' Miss Carter replied.

'Miss Carter,' Matty said, as they drove towards the station, 'Father wants me to learn, doesn't he?'

'Yes,' Miss Carter said.

'As much as I can?'

'As much as you're capable of.'

'And then?'

'And then you will be able to choose what you want to do with your life, how you can best be useful.'

Miss Carter began gathering up her hand luggage.

'Like Mother?' Matty said, turning the word 'useful' over in her head.

'Yes. But perhaps also a bit like your father.'

'Father said it wasn't right for women to want to be doctors.'

Mr Day opened the carriage door. Arthur waited politely for Miss Carter to get out before him.

Miss Carter sat and mused. She sighed. 'It's curious, isn't it? Nobody much minds if women work their fingers to the bone.' She smiled at Arthur. 'Nobody will protest about Eliza going out to service, and even the kindliest employers will work her from dawn till dark.'

'Eliza can do it,' Arthur said proudly. 'Eliza's no weakling.'

'I believe you,' said Miss Carter. 'But what if Eliza had wanted to drive an engine?'

'Eliza?' grinned Arthur. Mr Day chortled. 'Driving engines is men's work,' Arthur said.

Why? Matty wondered. Why were some things men's work and other things women's work? Did it always have to be that way?

Miss Carter shook her head. She got out of the carriage. Matty and Arthur followed. They were early for the train. Arthur said goodbye and ran off to the yard. Matty and Miss Carter found a seat on the platform.

Before long, the huge and mighty engine could be seen coming down the line towards them, great clouds of steam hissing and billowing all about it. The noise, as it approached, was tremendous.

'Such power!' Miss Carter cried. Majestically, the train clanked and squealed to a halt. 'No wonder men are proud of their achievements. Who would have thought all this was possible thirty years ago?'

They stepped up into the carriage. The seats were luxuriously padded. The brass fittings shone. Matty sat opposite Miss Carter, struck silent by the awesomeness of the great train and the great adventure that lay before her. Now Matty understood the way Nellie had felt. The train *was* a sort of heaving, hissing, iron monster of a horse and she was sitting inside it. Surely, it wasn't natural. You couldn't pat it or feed it sugar lumps.

But it was immensely exciting.

Miss Carter looked at her brightly. 'We live in an age of such progress, such improvement,' she said. 'None of us knows what we can do or where it will end. Who knows? Perhaps we will see stranger things yet than girls driving engines and becoming doctors.'

Then there was the noise of the engine and the rush of the steam.

'We're moving!' Matty cried. 'We're off!'

Further Reading

Now that you have read **The Doctor's Daughter**, you might like to read some other books about life in Victorian times. You might like to read other novels, true stories, or general information books. Here is a selection of the books available.

Fiction

Berlie Doherty	**Street Child,** *Puffin Books (1994)*
Leon Garfield	**John Diamond,** *Puffin Books (1995)*
Jill Paton Walsh	**Grace,** *Puffin Books (1993)*
Philippa Pearce	**Tom's Midnight Garden,** *Puffin Books (1995)*
Philip Pullman	**Spring-Heeled Jack,** *Corgi Yearling Books,* *Transworld Publishers (1991)*

Non-fiction

Clare Chandler	**Victorians,** *in the* **History Makers** *series* *Wayland Books (1994)*
David Evans	**How We Used To Live,** **Victorians Early And Late** *A & C Black (1993)*
Katrina Siliprandi	**Victorian Transport,** *in the* **Victorian Life** *series* *Wayland Books (1995)*